The First Day of Winter

For Will, Jane, and Ian

No part of this publication may be reproduced,
stored in a retrieval system, or transmitted in any
form or by any means, electronic, mechanical,
photocopying, recording, or otherwise, without
written permission of the publisher.
For information regarding permission, write to
Henry Holt and Company, LLC, 115 West 18th
Street, New York, NY 10011.

ISBN-13: 978-0-439-90878-8
ISBN-10: 0-439-90878-7

12 11 10 9 8 7 6 5 4 3 2 1   6 7 8 9 10 11/0

Printed in the U.S.A.   23

First Scholastic paperback printing,
November 2006

The illustrations were created using colored cotton fiber, hand-cut stencils, and squeeze bottles.
Book design by Denise Fleming and David Powers

The First Day of Winter

Denise Fleming

SCHOLASTIC INC.

New York Toronto London Auckland Sydney
Mexico City New Delhi Hong Kong Buenos Aires

December

Sunday	Monday	Tuesday	Wednesday	Thursday	Friday	Sat
					4	5
	1	2	3	10	11	
7	8	9	16	17	18	
14	15 ○	16	23 ◑	24		
	(21)	22	30 ●			
28	29					

First Day of Winter

Christmas Eve

On the **first** day of winter

my best friend gave to me…

...a red cap with a gold snap.

On the **second** day of winter
my best friend gave to me
2 bright blue mittens
and a red cap with a gold snap.

On the **third** day of winter
my best friend gave to me
3 striped scarves,
2 bright blue mittens,
and a red cap with a gold snap.

On the **fourth** day of winter
my best friend gave to me
4 prickly pinecones,
3 striped scarves,
2 bright blue mittens,
and a red cap
with a gold snap.

On the **fifth** day of winter
my best friend gave to me
5 birdseed pockets,
4 prickly pinecones,
3 striped scarves,
2 bright blue mittens,
and a red cap with a gold snap.

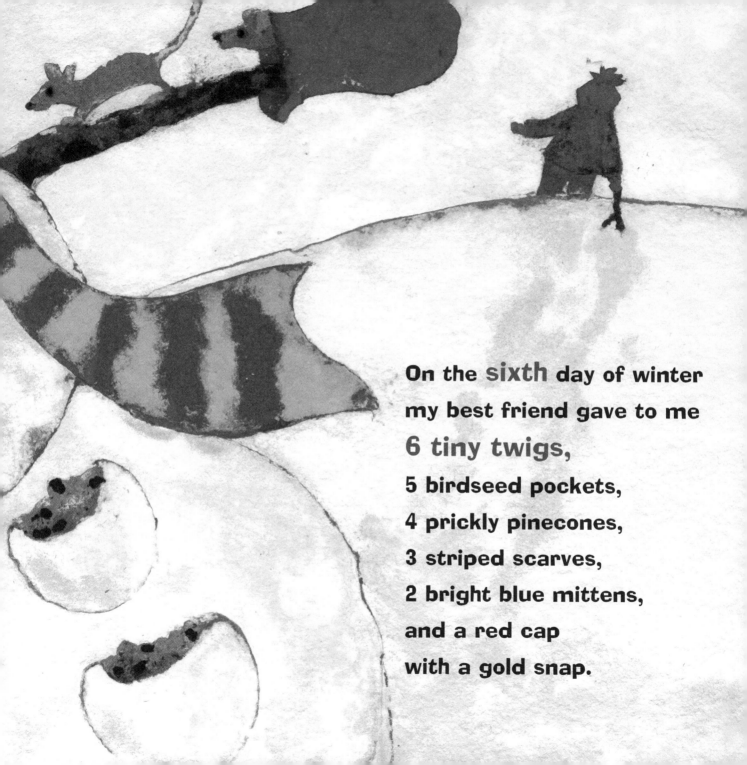

On the **sixth** day of winter
my best friend gave to me
6 tiny twigs,
5 birdseed pockets,
4 prickly pinecones,
3 striped scarves,
2 bright blue mittens,
and a red cap
with a gold snap.

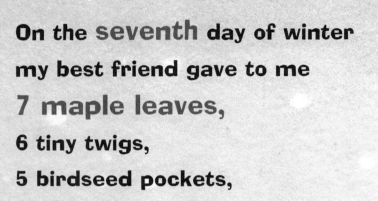

On the **seventh** day of winter
my best friend gave to me
7 maple leaves,
6 tiny twigs,
5 birdseed pockets,
4 prickly pinecones,
3 striped scarves,
2 bright blue mittens,
and a red cap with a gold snap.

On the **eighth** day of winter
my best friend gave to me
8 orange berries,
7 maple leaves,
6 tiny twigs,
5 birdseed pockets,
4 prickly pinecones,
3 striped scarves,
2 bright blue mittens,
and a red cap with a gold snap.

On the **ninth** day of winter
my best friend gave to me
9 big black buttons,
8 orange berries,
7 maple leaves,
6 tiny twigs,
5 birdseed pockets,
4 prickly pinecones,
3 striped scarves,
2 bright blue mittens,
and a red cap
with a gold snap.

On the **tenth** day of winter
my best friend gave to me
10 salty peanuts,
9 big black buttons,
8 orange berries,
7 maple leaves,
6 tiny twigs,
5 birdseed pockets,
4 prickly pinecones,
3 striped scarves,
2 bright blue mittens,
and a red cap
with a gold snap!